EARLY BIRD
STORIES

George and the New Craze

Early ★ Reader

First American edition published in 2019 by Lerner Publishing Group, Inc.

An original concept by Alice Hemming
Copyright © 2020 Alice Hemming

Illustrated by Kimberley Scott

First published by Maverick Arts Publishing Limited

Maverick
arts publishing

Licensed Edition
George and the New Craze

Lerner Publications Company
A division of Lerner Publishing Group, Inc.
241 First Avenue North
Minneapolis, MN 55401 USA

For reading levels and more information, look up this title at
www.lernerbooks.com.

Main body text set in Mikado. Typeface provided by HVD Fonts.

Library of Congress Cataloging-in-Publication Data

Names: Hemming, Alice, author. | Scott, Kimberley, illustrator.
Title: George and the new craze / by Alice Hemming ; illustrated by Kimberley
    Scott.
Description: Minneapolis : Lerner Publications, [2019] | Series: Early bird readers.
    Green (Early bird stories) | "The original picture book text for this story has
    been modified by the author to be an early reader." | Originally published in
    Horsham, West Sussex by Maverick Arts Publishing Ltd. in 2017.
Identifiers: LCCN 2018043752 (print) | LCCN 2018052753 (ebook) |
    ISBN 9781541561618 (eb pdf) | ISBN 9781541542068 (lb : alk. paper)
Subjects: LCSH: Readers (Primary) | Zoo animals—Juvenile literature. |
    Collectors and collecting—Juvenile literature.
Classification: LCC PE1119 (ebook) | LCC PE1119 .H4774 2019 (print) |
    DDC 428.6/2—dc23

LC record available at https://lccn.loc.gov/2018043752

Manufactured in the United States of America
1-45391-39007-11/9/2018

EARLY BIRD STORIES

George
and the
New Craze

Alice Hemming

Illustrated by
Kimberley Scott

Lerner Publications ◆ Minneapolis

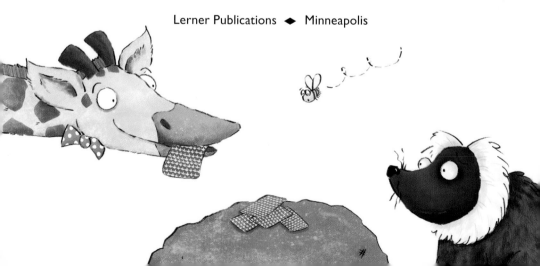

There was a new craze at the wildlife park. Everyone had cards with pictures of people on them!

The penguins had a full set of
People Cards.

George had three People Cards.
He was very happy with them—
even though two of the cards
were the same.

Gilbert

Gilbert is a truck driver. He also plays the drums in a band.

Gilbert

Gilbert is a truck driver. He also plays the drums in a band.

Sonia

Sonia is a hairdresser, and she loves to sing karaoke.

Sid had one card.

It was a rare card.

"What are People Cards for?"
Sid asked.

"I don't know," said George.

George and Sid tried to make a tower.

That didn't work.

They tried to play Snap.

That didn't work.

They put the cards in a big book.

There were lots of gaps.

They needed more cards.

"Shall we look for more
People Cards?" said George.

"No," said Sid. He liked his
one rare card.

George found a card.

It was a bit dirty, so he cleaned it up.

George bumped into Toni.

Toni was also looking for cards.

"Shall we share our cards?"
said George.

So they did.

So did Gus.

And Mo and Max.

And Minnie.

All together, they had lots of cards.

They made a big tower.

They played lots of games of Snap.

But they needed one more card to
fill up the book.

"I will share my rare card," said Sid.

Gilbert
Gilbert is a truck driver. He also plays the drums in a band.

Alice
Alice is an author. She likes rainy days.

Filippo
Filippo is a librarian. He has traveled to hundreds of different countries.

Clara
Clara is a schoolgirl. Her favorite animal is a platypus.

Mara
Mara is a horse rider. She loves to ride and care for her horses.

The Queen
The queen wears a shiny crown. She enjoys summer garden parties.

Sonia
Sonia is a hairdresser, and she loves to sing karaoke.

Rajit
Rajit is a veterinary surgeon. He bakes a lovely raspberry cheesecake.

Tommy
Tommy is a little boy. He rides his bike super-fast.

Babette
Babette is a security guard. Her favorite color is green.

Steve
Steve is a publisher. He wears extremely colorful shirts.

Kimberley
Kimberley is an illustrator. She likes to do yoga and stand on her head.

Everyone was happy. Sid was glad he had shared his card.

"Come and show the penguins!" said George.

But the penguins had finished with
People Cards.

They had started a new craze. Marbles!

Quiz

1. What is the first new craze at the wildlife park?
   a) Hats
   b) People Cards
   c) Marbles

2. Who has the rare card?
   a) George
   b) Sid
   c) Toni

3. What color is the rare card?
   a) Gold
   b) Blue
   c) Pink

4. How many cards are there altogether?
   a) One
   b) Three
   c) One hundred

5. What game do they play with
   the cards?
   a) Snap
   b) Happy families
   c) Guess the card

COLOR		GRL
Purple	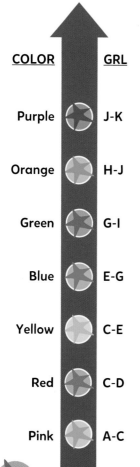	J-K
Orange		H-J
Green		G-I
Blue		E-G
Yellow		C-E
Red		C-D
Pink		A-C

EARLY BIRD STORIES™

Leveled for Guided Reading

Early Bird Stories have been edited and leveled by leading educational consultants to correspond with guided reading levels. The levels are assigned by taking into account the content, language style, layout, and phonics used in each book.